The author was a primary school teacher for many years working in the West Midlands, where she lives with her husband, Paul, and where she has lived all her life. Now retired, she enjoys walking every day in Sutton Park with Jazz. Anne has always had rescue dogs in her life, having grown up with the family one and having owned three dogs herself. All are special and have their own personalities… and Jazz is no exception!

JAZZ'S WINDOW

Anne Blackmore

AUSTIN MACAULEY PUBLISHERS™
LONDON • CAMBRIDGE • NEW YORK • SHARJAH

A CIP catalogue record for this title is available from the British Library.

ISBN 9781528915700 (Paperback)
ISBN 9781528929509 (ePub e-book)

www.austinmacauley.com

First Published (2020)
Austin Macauley Publishers Ltd
25 Canada Square
Canary Wharf
London
E14 5LQ

To Paul, who had the original inspiration for this story.

I would like to acknowledge Ray and Corinne Burrows for helping me with the illustrations. Also, my heartful thanks to Beehive Illustrations.

This is Jazz.

PICTURE 2

Jazz lives in a big, white house on a busy main road.

He lives there with his owners, who he calls his 'mummy' and 'daddy'. Of course they aren't really his mummy and daddy

They looked more like this:

or maybe this

or even this!

This is Jazz's window. It is his look out post on the world.
While Jazz's owners are out at work he sits looking out of his
beautiful window. It has stained glass panels high up.

He sees Mrs Bellman taking Charlie to school. She pushes baby Sarah along in the buggy. Jazz puts his front paws on the low windowsill and barks at them as they pass his strong, black gates.

Then a delivery van arrives next door. What's this? They are having
a new fridge-freezer.
It is Jazz's job to bark loudly at the delivery people even though
they are not at his house!

For a while all goes quiet and Jazz settles down for a snooze on the landing beneath his window. An hour or so ticks by and Jazz decides it is time for a scratch and a stretch. He places his front paws forwards, leans his head down and sticks his bottom in the air, bending his back and pressing his tummy to the floor. He has a shake and trots back over to his window.

Jazz is in luck! The neighbour, Mrs Forrest, is just coming out to her car. Jazz wags his tail and barks excitedly! Mrs Forrest glances up at the window, where she can just make out Jazz's outline. As she gets into her car and drives out, Jazz looks along the road for signs of any more activity. There is nothing doing so he decides to head downstairs and check out the biscuits which he left in his bowl earlier.

Next he wanders into the lounge, circles in his bed and curls up for another sleep – but he has one eye open!

Jazz naps happily through the rest of the morning but then…
Suddenly there is the sound of the letterbox being flipped up and
letters tumbling into the porch. As quick as a flash jazz is up
and zooming upstairs to his window. Paws on the sill, he barks his
loudest yet at the postman, who is walking back down the drive.
This is Jazz's favourite barking opportunity! He continues to watch
carefully as post is delivered next door.

Jazz casts his gaze back over his front drive. A pigeon has arrived and is pecking at the ground, head bobbing back and forth, as it potters along, unaware that it is being watched. Jazz fixes his stare on the bird – if only he could get out; what a chase he would have! Moments later the pigeon takes off and flies into the big copper beech tree and Jazz sits quietly surveying the scene.

Time passes. It must be nearly time for mummy to arrive home. Jazz waits patiently, the ticking of the grandfather clock marking the time. At last Jazz hears the sound of a car turning into the drive – can it be? YES it's definitely mummy home! As the key turns in the front door lock, Jazz is halfway down the stairs. His tail wags furiously and it's walkie time. Off to the park goes Jazz and his window waits.
Tomorrow is another day!